*Printed
For
Quixote Press
by*
BRENNAN PRINTING
*100 Main Street
Deep River, Iowa 52222*
515-595-2000

My Very First . . . . .

by

Baldwin, Leslie
Belcher, Jason
Belcher, Jonathan
Belcher, Jamie
Bergstrom, Haddi
Bernand, Curry
Boughton, Ryan
Brockett, Bo
Brockett, Jeff
Burrell, Nina
Carkhuff, Arthur
Champagne, Tim
Christofferson, Amanda
Chubb, Jennifer
Cordts, Virginia
Corwin, Jeff
Dietsch, Brandon
Donlan, Amanda
Douglas, Dustin
Engel, Kellie
Faaborg, Beverly Parks
Faust, Rebecca
George, LaShawna
Hartman, Janelle
Herbst, Stacey
Hood, Kim
Judd, Shawn
King, Reagan
Meyer, Kimberly
Nelson, Sarah
Nupp, James
Patrick, Matthew
Peterson, Zach
Phillips, Michelle
Piper, Damion
Russell, Jennifer
Ryner, Eric
Sacora, Bobbie
Sawyer, Lea
Smith, Sarah
Sturdevant, Sarah
Sturms, Robert
Sudbeck, Sara
Turley, Brandie
Tutt, Jason
Wallace, Katie
Walz, Chris
Wasson, Jason
Wilson, Holly
Wisner, Daniel
Wordsworth, Stephanie

Quixote Press
R.R. #4, Box 33B
Blvd. Station
Sioux City, Iowa
51109

© *1992 by Beverly Parks Faaborg*

All rights reserved. No part of this book may be reproduced or transmitted in any form or by any means, electronic or mechanical, including photocopying, recording or by any informational storage or retrieval system, except by a reviewer who may quote brief passages in a review to be printed in a magazine or newspaper without permission in writing from the publisher. For information contact Bruce Carlson, Quixote Press, R.R. #4, Box 33B, Blvd. Station, Sioux City, Iowa 51109.

QUIXOTE PRESS
Bruce Carlson
R.R. #4, Box 33B
Blvd. Station
Sioux City, Iowa
51109

PRINTED IN U.S.A.

DEDICATION

— to all the people who made it happen.

Table of Contents

FORWORD 9
PREFACE................................... 11
CHAPTERS
    I   13
    II   19
    III   23
    IV   27
    V   31
    VI   35
    VII   39
    VIII   43
    IX   47
    X   51
    XI   55
    XII   59
    XIII   63
    XIV   65
    XV   67
    XVI   69
    XVII   73
    XVIII   75
    XIX   77
    XX   79
    XXI   81
    XXII   83
    XXIII   85
    XXIV   87
    XXV   89
    XXVI   91
    XXVII   93
    XXVIII   95
    XXIX   97
    XXX   99

XXXI	103
XXXII	105
XXXIII	107
XXXIV	109
XXXV	111
XXXVI	115
XXXVII	119
XXXVIII	121
XXXIX	123
XL	125
XLI	129
XLII	133
XLIII	137
XLIV	141
XLV	143
XLVI	145
XLVII	149
XLVIII	151
XLIX	153
L	157
LI	161
EPILOGUE	165

FOREWORD

It'd be a rare person who could read MY VERY FIRST . . . without recognizing some of their own experiences from their own childhood. We've all gotten the bejammers scared out of us, done something real dumb or embarrassing, or ended up doing something we found out was a whole lot different than we expected.

These tales by and about children offer us fresh ways of looking at things, ways we've forgotten about as we busy ourselves doing things for the hundredth or thousandth time.

Professor Phil Hey
Briar Cliff College
Sioux City, Iowa

PREFACE

We all have some "first time" that we recall with a memory so sharp that it might as well have happened yesterday instead of back when it did, a lot more years ago then we'd like to think.

Maybe it was that first pair of new shoes . . . . or a stolen watermelon . . . . or a stolen kiss. It's hard not to smile sometimes when we think of those things.

MY VERY FIRST . . . . is a book by children of today, and about children of yesterday. It's about the first times these children of long ago did this or that. Some of the magic of those things can be found within these pages.

I

...... HOME IN THE COUNTRY

(Melva Dustman's story as told by Sarah Sturdevant)

I guess I was what you'd call an environmentalist when I was just a little shaver. I really did love living in our house out in the country on our little farm where I could explore the woods to my heart's content. It always hurt me when I saw anything out there in the woods get hurt 'cause I just figured the sun rose and set on my little brushy corner of the world.

The little creek that wandered through our place was the closest thing to a best friend back then. It wasn't long after we moved to that place that I discovered the creek.

Now that I think about it after a lot of years of livin', I'd have to admit that it was probably about as common a creek as a fellow could find. But at the time I just figured that creek was, without a doubt, a long stringy piece of magic that fell out of the sky right onto our new place.

I loved that creek. And, you know it's strange, but I kind of figured that creek loved me back, because it seemed of a mind not to leave our place. It'd twist and turn, doin' all sorts of things rather than to hurry on through our place on down to the neighbors.

Now, of course, I can understand those fancy college fellas who talk about erosion, hydraulics, and all that stuff. Back then, though, I just thought the creek didn't want to leave our place.

Goin' to the creek to find pretty rocks was one of my most favorite things to do.

The best way to find nice rocks worn smooth over the years was to wade around lookin' for 'em. Oh, Gosh!, but that water would be cold sometimes early in the summer. But havin' to put up with that cold cold water was simply the price I had to pay for those pretty rocks.

If I'd find a rock that wasn't real pretty, just an ordinary sort of rock, I'd pitch it over by some frogs

and make them jump in with a big hollow sounding KER . . . . PLOP.

Now and then I'd come across a rock that was nice and flat with rounded edges. The best ones would be a little thicker in the center than on the edges. When I found one of those I would have one real fine "skipping rock". These were rocks that would skip across the top of the water in the creek just like it was a bouncing rubber ball.

To get a rock to skip just right you had to hold it just right, hunker down a little bit just right, throw that thing so's it'd hit the water flat, and doing all that with a little spin to it.

When you'd come risin' up outta that throw and look about across the water, it was a real lot of fun. You could see that rock skipping along the top of the water just like it had no plans whatsoever to go 'round sinkin' like some old ordinary rock.

It was common knowledge that there was something in the makeup of girls that didn't allow us to skip a rock properly. But I proved them wrong.

Now that I've had a little time to think about it, I'll bet we skipped rocks better than the boys. Maybe it's lucky for boys that we girls found other things more fun to do.

Also, now that I've had time to think about it, I really suspect that I was right after all. Maybe it really was true that the creek hated to leave our place. Maybe that didn't have anything to do with hydraulics, and all that stuff, after all. Maybe that creek did love me 'most as much as I loved it.

II

......FAMILY MOVE

(Dick Lloyd's story as told by Jeff Corwin)

hen my Ma told me we were moving, I was really scared. I wondered why we had to leave our regular home near my Grandma's.

The big folks kept talking about something called "The Depression", but they might as well have been talking about a hole in the ground as far as I was concerned.

I didn't know if The Depression was something I'd have to turn the crank on like I did the ice cream churn or the milk separator, or if it was something I'd end up with the chore of having to feed every night. It all seemed pretty confusing to me.

As it turned out, I didn't have to turn any crank on The Depression or even have to feed it every night like a dog or a cat. But it did make us move. That made it pretty serious and pretty scarey.

We didn't have a place to live before we moved, so we took our belongings in a big old flatbed truck. We ended up moving in with my Aunt for a while until my Pa could find work.

Moving might have meant a promise of a better life for Ma and Pa, but to me it meant having to face a scary new school.

I was real bashful in the new school. I wouldn't read aloud and couldn't really do the work. All the big folks got their heads together and came up with the idea that I should start in the first grade again.

At first I wasn't sure a fresh start was what I really wanted, but Ma talked me into it. She said it was like having a chance at a nice shiny apple without some scraggly old bite out of it, or a new pair of shoes with the store-bought smell still in 'em.

Ma was always pretty good at talking me into stuff that way, and I fell for it, hook, line, and sinker.

III

. . . . . . RICKETY OLD EMPTY HOUSE

(Gladys Harper's story as told by Dustin Douglas)

"Once there was a ghost who lived to get little kids . . . . "

We little kids shuddered as we heard one ghost story after another on a dreary and rainy day. The wind . . . . or was it a ghost? . . . . rattled the loose boards on the empty old house on Grandpa's homestead.

The old house had been built by my grandfather who had a deed signed by President Polk.

There were lots of nooks and crannies among the steep stairs which made the old house perfect for hide and seek games. Who knew what was lurking in the passageways that seemed to be built for the express purpose of scaring children?

Since there were things stored in some rooms, we kids lined the boxes up and played church; we had rows of pews. Another day, these boxes became forts where captured Indian princesses were put by Indian braves.

Someone had made a ball by winding white twine around a wad of cloth. What a great time we had throwing it over the old house roof! We'd yell

"Andy Over!!" as our team threw the ball over the weather-beaten old roof. If the ball came back down on our side instead of going over, we yelled, "Pig Tail!!" Of course, if the ball went all the way over and was caught by the other team, they'd sneak around to tag us before we could get away.

Sometimes as I look into the clouds on a warm summer afternoon I ask myself why none of us ever questioned that business of "Andy Over", and "Pig Tail." It was never "Fred Over!!" or "Cow Tail". I guess we just figured that's all it could be and had been since the beginning of time.

Ah, those memories of Grandfather's old rickety empty house. I wonder if those noises we heard really were ghosts.

IV

・・・・・・ HOUSE BUILDING

(Catherine Herbst's story as told by Stacey Herbst)

talians make a party out of everything. With Italians, parties are parties and things that aren't parties are parties, too. So, of course, it was one giant party there at our place when my Pa built our first house.

There were all kinds of excitment in the family as we figured we'd have rooms for everyone in the whole family.

And, believe me, that possibility was mighty attractive to us. We had gotten so crowded that when one guy rolled over in bed, everyone in it had to do likewise.

And you can sure bet there wasn't anyone of us who complained about having to work on the house. Not only did Ma and Pa do a terrible lot of work on that house, but so did all us kids. Then, besides that, there were a whole bunch of our friends who still carried the dust of Italy on their boots who helped.

There's still talk in the family about all the good Italian dinners and the shouts to and fro as these big strong men worked putting up the rafters, and the walls.

A real special part of this new house was that it would be having a real live inside bathroom. It was going to be our first bathroom, and none of us could wait to say our last good-bye to that old outhouse in the back.

My Pa said I could pick out the color for my own room, so I thought and thought about that. Should it be white, green, pink, or blue?

I often wondered about one thing. I would think about if later owners of that house ever did any remodeling, and found the good luck penny we cemented into each wall all those years and years ago.

V

...... HOUSE MOVING

(Berniece Gerdes's story as told by Brandie Turley)

e had a parade in our town one summer. It wasn't a very long one, (just one thing was in it) but it lasted for a full month.

Well, maybe it really wasn't a parade, but it looked like one in some ways. It went really slowly down the street and had an audience watching it.

Actually, what it was, was our house being moved to a different lot.

This parade had quite an audience when it had to turn off our street onto Virginia Street and made that sharp turn.

Folks had never seen a house perched up on a string of farm wagons before. A big old truck was hooked onto it to pull it along. They'd pull the thing a few inches, then stop and look it all over to see if everything was hanging together.

Every day the couple that was moving the house had to take down some overhead wires, and then put them back up again after the house had gone through. All that took so much time that on some days the house hardly moved at all.

The people who moved our house lived right in it while they were moving it. Each day their living quarters would be a few feet further down the road than it was when they started out that day.

All that caused kind of a strange thing. You see, we had never had a dog in our house. Ma wouldn't let us have one inside. But, those people who were moving the house had a dog, and they kept him right there in our house. We couldn't have one, but they did.

Not only did they have that dog in the house, but it actually had puppies while it was living in there.

I was in hopes that after they got the house all moved we could have a dog in the house, especially after that one had pups in there.

But, there was no such luck, we still had to leave our dog outside even after the house finally got to our new lot.

VI

. . . . . . CELLAR

(Dorothy Hoschek's story as told by Sarah A. Nelson)

hat is dark, and scary? I'll tell you what was . . . . . the cellar in our house when I was five.

To get to our cellar, I had to open a closet door in the dining room, lift up the trap door to that awful place, and then walk down creaky steps.

I was afraid of that dark hole and just knew that all kinds of creatures and varmints were waiting to jump on me down there. My friends all had tales of a cellar they had heard about that had a snake in it!

After that, I just knew that ours did too, except, in our cellar, the snake had multiplied and had a big family in my cellar, so I made the trip as fast as I could.

The cellar was cold, and it was damp. I could feel spider webs hitting my face as I reluctantly put one foot in front of the other on my way down there.

Maybe there could be ghosts down there....... I tightened my grip on the kerosene lamp which I carried in one hand while I held onto the wooden railing with the other one.

The walls were covered with shelves full of canned vegetables, crocks of sauerkraut, smoked meat, dried apples, and potatoes. This little dungeon-like room smelled of all those things, and musty on top of that.

It was deathly quiet..... except when something scampered in a dark corner. I much preferred quiet to scampering!!

What a relief to scurry up the steep stairs once more into the cheerfulness and safety of the dining room.

Nothing bad had happened this time during my seven minute trip, but . . . . . who knew about the next time.

VII

...... OUTHOUSE

(Laurence Coen's Story as told by Damion Piper)

uthouses ...... every home had one back from the house, usually out back. We called them privies or toilets, or described them according to the number of holes.

Some outhouses were private one-holers, but some were two-holers. On occasion, you'd find one with a third, and smaller facility for a child. The whole

family could go at once, I guess.

Our little outhouse was wood and had little windows cut out, high up on the side. There was a vent cut in the door in the shape of a crescent moon. Some outhouses had tin roofs, but ours didn't.

Oftentimes, outhouses were painted to match the house, and even equipped with screen doors. Some times there would be wooden lids over the bench-like seats. Ours just had a plain old board with a bottom-pinching crack in it.

In the summer the flies and the smell could get pretty awful, so we'd keep a bucket of lime on hand to sprinkle down in the pit from time to time.

Sometimes there was toilet paper, but often we had only corn cobs, a catalog, or some other substitute.

We used the pit in our old outhouse to get rid of junk, too. Glass bottles, broken china, and other household castoffs got tossed in there.

The outhouses in our neighborhood were considered fair game for pranksters, especially at Halloween.

Pushing over outhouses was pretty much a boy's pastime. And, of course, every time an outhouse got pushed over, you had to hear a whole lot of outhouse-pushing-over stories. The best ones were the ones that told about outhouses getting pushed over that had someone in them.

VIII

. . . . . . CHICKEN KILLING

(Helen Coen's story as told by Zach Peterson)

The first time I ever helped kill a chicken, I was only six years old.

The thing I hated most was the smell. There is just no escaping it, a dead wet chicken smells like a dead wet chicken, and it was awful.

But, before we got to that awful stage in the whole thing, there were other awful things to do first. In that sordid business of doin' in a chicken, you have to do things in the right order, and that's what we did.

First, there was the terrible matter of making a choice about which one to do.

And, then, of course, someone has to hold the unlucky critter so the other fellow can cut the head off. I felt just about how I figured the chicken must have felt when I found out that my job was going to be just that . . . holding onto the fluttering, squawking thing so someone else could man the axe.

Holding that noisy clatterin'-around chicken who was jumping in all directions at once was bad. The only thing worse was to have to feel its icky skin. All in all, I don't know who felt the worse, me or the chicken.

By this time I figured things were about as bad as they could get, but I was wrong. They were fixin' to get a whole lot worse. No sooner did that chicken go one way while his head went another, but what he got to jumpin' around like I'd never seen a chicken jump before. He jumped higher and faster than I thought a chicken had it in him to do. And, all the while, there was blood spurtin' around and splattering over everything, and squawking!! Now, I really never have figured out how that animal could be squwaking that way. But he was, and didn't seem to mind the least little bit he had no head to do it with!

Finally, after an eternity, the chicken laid there in the grass, still as could be.

We had to pick that critter up by his icky feet and plunge him into some real hot water. Out of that old black pot of water came the biggest and awfulest stinky cloud of steam you'd ever hope to see. Suddenly the whole world seemed to be full of the smell of hot wet feathers.

Well, of course, there was no longer any hope at all that things, could get any worse. This had to be the very bottom!

But it wasn't. It got a whole lot worse. Not only did we have to hold that naked chicken over a fire to singe the little hairly feathers off, and we got treated to the delicious smell of burnt feathers, but we were treated to the opportunity to take his insides out. I'm not even going to talk about that.

But I did learn one important thing from helping with that job that day. I learned that I would never, never . . . . I mean never butcher another chicken again.

IX

. . . . . . THRESHING

(James Hodges's story as told by Jason Wasson)

It couldn't be! That machine couldn't possibly be that big! There was no way my young mind was going to believe all those wheels, belts, chains, bins, and all could be just one machine. But it was. That monster that looked like it came out of one of my really really bad dreams was actually driving up our lane and coming into our barn lot, all accompained with creaks, and groans, and puffs of smoke and steam, just like that terrible terrible creature that had invaded my sleep the other night.

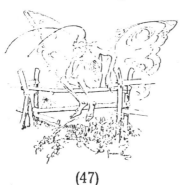

I think my mouth must have dropped down to about where my chest usually was as I stood there by the door watching that threshing machine come lumbering into our place.

Oh, I'd seen big machines before. I thought that Pa's corn picker was pretty good sized . . . and hay racks, why hay racks were awfully big even without a load of hay on them; but this thing!

There I stood, afraid to get any farther from the safety of the house, and yet afraid to take my eyes off of that monster for fear that it might sneak up and eat up the house in a bite or two.

But it didn't. That big old creaky thing turned out to be pretty tame after all, especially after I had retreated to where I could watch it out of the kitchen window.

Soon I lost my fear of that machine as the farm became lost in the shouts of men, all getting ready to do the threshing. Mixed up with that were the women all talking to each other as they began to turn covered baskets and mysterious packages into pies, fruit jars full of beautiful red berries and other canned stuff. Mountains of breads and desserts seemed to rise up out of the very soil at our little farm, along with oceans of delicious gravy, the kind with little lumps that made farmer's gravy so much better than any other in the whole world.

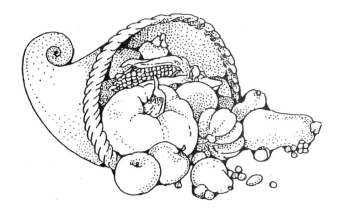

Even the cats and the dogs seemed to catch the spirit of the day, and rushed from one thing to the other, just like all the urchins that appeared out of wagons and buggys in our drive.

I went with a couple of the older kids to the field to help set up little teepee-like things out of the bundles of oats. Men with strong muscles threw those bundles up onto a wagon, where others moved them to THE MACHINE. Like all threshing days, it was the hottest day of the year, and the sweat made those men's backs glisten like they had been waxed and shined.

I almost lost track of time, but I knew the crew was there two or three days, each meal of each day, being a tremendous affair.

A few of the observers of the whole thing, the feathered ones with two legs didn't hang around to see the end of it all. They ended up in the pot to feed everybody. No sooner would dinner be over, but the women would start getting ready for the afternoon snacks that would be hauled to the field in wicker baskets. The good ladies would then rush back to the house to start getting ready for the big feed at supper.

The silence that fell over our farm after everybody had moved on to the next one was so heavy I thought things would never be the same again. But they were. And things went back to normal again . . . . until a year later when this unbelievably big machine came huffin' and puffin' down our lane and it was so big that . . . .

X

...... MILKING

(Mary Derby's story as told by Sarah Smith)

A couple of old pictures that show milking time on our farm make it seem almost like milking time was a leisure time activity. Folks were standing around smiling at the camera just as if they had all the time in the world to do that job.

But, those old photos don't tell all the truth. Milking time was leisure time just like mice chase cats.

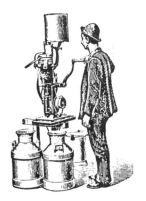

The day I was enlisted to help with milking I was given my very own milking stool to sit on. All it was was two short boards, one nailed crosswise on the other, but it was all mine, and I was proud as punch of that little stool.

I had watched the big folks milk of course, so had some idea of what to do from that. And, of course, I was given a crash course in the art of milking somewhere between my instructor doing the feeding and his running into another room in the barn to take care of the little calves.

So, I proceeded to get to it. After quite a bit of practice I found that on rare occasion I was able to even hit the bucket with a stream of milk now and then.

Having accomplished that small detail, I went on to develop the skill that I felt was the only one worth having, that being the ability to squirt a stream of milk and have the cat catch it in her mouth. That, to me, was what milking was all about.

The cat and I worked on that pretty diligently until we both got kicked out for being in the way.

No, that's not quite right. I was all in favor of milk. Well, maybe not in favor of milk so much as I was in favor of what would happen after we'd take the milk down into the celler in big crocks.

Before long the cream would rise to the top where we'd take it off with a cream skimmer and haul it up into the kitchen. The kitchen is where the magic would happen.

I still don't know how the magic worked, but that cream would turn into things that little girls could hardly stand to eat . . . . things like ice cream, mounds of rich yellow butter, and sinfully good stuff like whipped cream used to smother the life out of pumpkin pie.

XI

. . . . . . HOG BUTCHERING

(Purl Van Hemert's story as told by Jonathan Belcher)

h!, how I remember my very first butchering day.

I suppose I had been around on other hog butchering days before that, but I was probably kept inside with the other little kids.

But, this day, I got to help! If the truth were known, I'd probably been the best help if I'd stayed in the house again, out from under foot. But I thought I was helping the big folks a whole lot.

And, I sure didn't want to miss any of the excitement of the day. Folks would talk about The Big Day for a couple of days beforehand and then also for a couple of days after the day was gone and the big old black kettle would be put away.

They told me the hog weighed about two hundred pounds. I figured that would make about three of even some of the bigger boys there. And he looked like it too. I was having some trouble trying to see how all those folks were going to turn that big old critter into pork chops and hams.

I wasn't at all sure I felt very good about the part when they cut the critter's throat, but I guess that was part of the whole operation.

We had a huge black pot filled with water, stoked with a wood fire underneath of it. It was a cool fall day and clouds of steam would rise up out of that kettle as if it were going to fill the whole sky.

I thought, at first, the men were teasing me again when they told me they were going to shave the hog.

I had visions, of course, of the men breaking out a whole bunch of shaving mugs, and lathering the hog down to shave it like they did themselves with lather and a sharp razor.

Well, it wasn't quite that way. They didn't use any lather at all. They simply dipped the hog in that huge pot of hot water and scrapped all the hair off.

Things got kind of messy then as the men sorted out the stuff to keep and the stuff to throw away. I tended to think most of what I saw should be thrown away, but no one seemed to pay a whole lot of attention to my recommendations on that.

The whole operation seemed to be a strange combination of lots of water, men working and women scurrying around making sausage, and rendering lard.

Right there before my eyes what had just been a big old hog turned into piles of hams, roasts, pork chops and all those other goodies!

Off went the hams to the smoke house where they would hang, to be used later in the winter. Some of the meat got cooked right there, ready to be stored, all sealed over with lard down in the cellar.

Weeks or months later when those hams and cooked meat would be used while the winter wind blew around the corner of the house, we would remember the day when we did the butchering.

Seventy years later I can still recall "Butchering Days" as if they were just last week.

XII

. . . . . . COVERED WAGON

(Audra Miller's story as told by Bo Brockett)

t the turn of the century my father homesteaded some land. That, of course, meant we had to move all our belongings to the new place.

We not only had to take all the things we'd need there, but we had to take a lot of stuff we'd need along the way for our eating and sleeping.

The wagon was chuck full of things by the time we left, and there certainly wasn't room for any unnecessary things like games or fancy clothes.

Our wagon was like all the covered wagons of the time. It had long hook-like things to form a frame for the roof which was nothing more than a big piece of canvas.

At night we camped, making our beds on the grass beside the wagon. We three kids thought it was fun to sleep that way, and to cook our meals over campfires, and to ford the river.

And, then there was the train. I didn't even know we were near a railroad when we pulled up to camp in that little grove of trees. But we had.

I think I felt the ground tremble just a little bit under my thin blanket even before I heard the chug-chug-chug of the train.

But, then I head it! It was the most magnificant thing I'd ever heard before that, or since. It came roaring into my small life, changing it forever.

Even before the caboose disappeared before my astonished eyes, I had made a decision. I decided that riding a train would be the most wonderful thing that could ever happen to me.

That night, as I lay on the suddenly still ground, I dreamt of what it must feel like to ride a train, to be part of such a thing that could come roaring out of the night, then disappear again.

But the reality of homesteading brought me back to earth pretty quickly.

They snuffed out those flights of fancy about such exotic things as train rides as I found myself with the chore of having to collect dried cow chips to burn in the cookstove in our new home.

I discovered a rather interesting thing about life as a homesteader. I discovered that collecting chow chips wasn't nearly as exciting as other things I could think of ..... things like riding a train that roared in out of the night, then out of the life of a scared little girl lying on the ground by a covered wagon.

XIII

...... SLEIGH RIDE

*(Deloris Willard's story as told
by Stephanie Wordsworth)*

hat is it about the magic of a child's thoughts? What is it that brings visions to children as they learn of this world of ours?

I think that as I recall of how it was on my very first sleigh ride.

I remember the horses snorting in the cold. Even in their nervous dancing with the clouds of steam coming out of their flared and redened nostrils, they seemed to enjoy knowing there was a sleigh behind them.

And, the bells, those bells weren't just sleigh bells. There was no doubt in my mind but what they were actually happy, jingling with a special feeling, knowing we were on our way to Grandma's.

And, that hot chocolate that warmed us all up there at Grandma's still warms me today as I think of my first sleigh ride.

XIV

...... STREETCAR RIDE

(Dorothy Schoelkopf's story as told by Janelle Hartman)

"other, now may I pull the cord?" I teased over and over again. I wanted to be the one to signal the streetcar driver to let us off at Grandma's stop.

How I loved riding the streetcar! It should have run real quietly on those mirror-like rails, but it

didn't. The inside was filled with the noise and racket of many people all crowed together, people going to work, and those coming home from their labors. There were shoppers, kids, old folks and even a child or two sometimes.

The outside of the streetcar was filled with the noise of the old vehicle rattling back and forth on its frame, dogs in hot pursit, and so forth. All in all, it was an ideal way to travel.

The conductor was king of his little rolling kingdom, working his way from one end of it to the other, collecting a nickel from each of the passengers.

And, the best part was that I got to pull the signal cord when we got close to where we had to get off to go to Grandma's.

In that brief moment when I pulled that cord, I was in charge of that entire little kingdom.

XV

...... CAR RIDE

(Winifred Witte's story as told by Kellie Engel)

I was nervous, Mama was worried sick, and Papa was anxiously making arrangements for the trip.

Mama had discovered a lumpy knot on my rib and thought I had something bad. Old Doc Mott said I must have an X-ray in another town, so we were planning a trip in his car.

I was eight years old in 1918, and had never ridden in a car. I was double scared . . . afraid I had something real serious wrong with my rib, and also afraid of the new "horseless carriage."

Papa and Doc put me in the back seat while they rode up front. I wondered if it was going to be safe to ride in that contraption.

As we chugged along, I thought about what a strange thing this automobile was compared to a buggy. The sound of the motor scared me a little. And the horn! What a funny sound it made.

But, we made it and without any disasters along the way.

Both the rib and the car turned out to be alright.

XVI

...... MODEL T CAR

(John Wetherford's story as told by Ryan Boughton)

There weren't any such things as drivers' licenses in 1930, so when I turned fifteen, I bought an old Model T Ford for the hefty sum of four dollars. It was a 1922 or 1923, one of the earliest models.

The car wasn't much to look at, and I really didn't think it was all that great, but it was all mine. Actually, the thing was little more than a chassis and an engine.

Since there wasn't even a seat, I sat on the gas tank to drive. It wasn't even a real color; simply a natural rust sort of like iron.

I don't know what the problem was, but I discovered I

had to stop every now and then to put water in the radiator. Since that proved to be more "now's" than "then's", I ended up putting a box on the back, and carrying it full of jugs of water.

I did all the things that young fellows do with cars, of course. But, I soon found my first love was racing.

Oh, we had organized races and all, with prize money at some of them. We even had a regular race track, regular at that time, anyway.

Our race track was called Oak Stubblefield, and was square as a checkerboard, square shaped, and a mile around.

That track was hardly deserving of the name. It was dirt, rutted, and rough as it could be. And at speeds up to sixty miles an hour on a rutted old track, you just never knew what part was going to be flying off next.

At each of those square corners was a man to help get the car around it, and to pick up any pieces of the car or driver that happened to get left there. If you thought something was going to happen, you just bailed out and hoped you hit right.

I did most of my racing for money, but the purses were

so little, it hardly counted at all. The most I ever won was thirty or forty dollars.

After my racing career ended, I took the car apart and split it up with a friend of mine. I kept the radiator, the magneto, and the magnets pin. I don't know what he did with his parts, but I put mine on another old car and started all over again.

XVII

. . . . . . FAST CAR

(Curtis Bernand's story as told by Curry Bernand)

y mother called my car the fastest car in Green Rock, Illinois.

She really had two reasons for doing that. One was that the speedometer was permanantly stuck at 80 mph, even when it was doing nothing but dropping grease all over me as I worked endless hours on that car.

The other reason she called it that was because the car wouldn't run at all, much less 80 mph.

But, I didn't care if she made fun of my car. It was all mine, and paid for with my money. After all, I only paid fifty dollars for that gem, and I knew that it had the makings of being one fine running car if I could ever get it off the blocks I used to work on that thing.

When I finally did get that old car going, I even fixed the speedometer so it worked properly.

That, of course, ended that car's career at being the fastest car in Green Rock, and my mother's always making fun of it.

XVIII

. . . . . . NEIGHBOR

(Gerald Sacora's story as told by Bobbie Sacora)

The very first neighbor I ever had, or at least remember was an old maid Bohemian lady who scared the very bejammers off of me.

For some unknown reason this old gal took it upon herself to teach me to eat with my right hand.

Well, I was just learning to eat at all at the time, and was having a bad time of it trying to get that food to my mouth with my left hand that I wanted to use.

Miss Jones told me that she was my guardian angel to help me learn to eat right. Well, you can be sure I didn't look upon that busybody as some kind of guardian angel. I figured she was some kind of pestering witch instead.

Like I say, I could hardly eat with my left hand, much less do it all backwards to satisfy someone who would sit there and watch me eat. It didn't help that I was scared stiff of that woman, either.

I'd spill soup all over the front of my shirt or else go hungry by not eating it at all. Sometimes I had to do that since being rude or mouthy to one's elders was not allowed, regardless of the reason.

XIX

. . . . . . GIANT FRIEND

**(Laura Kroeger-Manley story as
told by LaShawna George)**

When I was three years old I was almost three feet tall. My friend Bob was almost nine feet tall. Robert was the tallest man in the world and weighed four hundred, ninety five pounds. But to me, he was simply my friend.

Robert and I had a problem. I was too small to play games with the other kids, and he was too big.

(77)

So, we kind of got thrown together with similar problems. We ended up sitting on the steps together a lot and talking.

Robert could seldom go anywhere to visit because there simply weren't any beds or chairs anywhere else big enough for him to use. I was secretly kind of glad about that because that meant that he would be around for me to spend more time with.

There wasn't much of a future for Robert in our hometown, so eventually he joined a circus and people paid to see the "giant". I was sad that he was gone, and it made me feel bad that people might laugh at him.

When he died at only twenty two years old, it took four burial spaces for the casket. And, he took about that much space in my heart, too.

XX

. . . . . . BOY PROBLEMS

(Alice Billerbeck's story as told by Nina Burrell)

It was when I was only five years old and going to a two-story brick school house to kindergarten.

One of the things we had to do was to practice going down the fire escape from the second story down to the ground.

Our fire escape was a huge metal tube that was curved and real dark inside.

We girls didn't like to go in there, much less slide down all the way to the ground in that scary thing.

Well, if that wasn't bad enough, the boys found out pretty quickly that we were scared of that fire escape, and they would tease us unmercifully about that. They would tell us about all kinds of goblins and spooks inside that tube, knowing we'd be scared spitless to go down into it.

It's an awfully big world when you are only five years old and you're not real sure about anything,

much less scary things like big metal tubes that have scary curves in it, and in the dark, yet!

And then, to make it all the worse, these awful boys weren't content to make life difficult for us in school, but they would chase us home after school.

I found out pretty early that boy problems aren't fun problems to have.

XXI

. . . . . . FIGHT

(Lyle Graham's story as told by Shawn Judd)

wo little boys rolled around and around on the school yard, while a circle of kids watched.

I was one of those boys. Over and over we tumbled while muffled grunts occasionally floated up out of the tussle.

My opponent and I both had our eyes on the same girl in our class. Apparently neither of us had enough sense to wonder what her preference might be. We both stumbled along, just sort of assuming she was the prize over which we were fighting, and that she'd go along with our goofy ideas.

We both knew the stakes were high. Not only were we fighting for the pretty little prize, but we also knew the winner would be a hero, at least for the afternoon.

So, we both got into that fight with both feet, grabbing shirts, tearing buttons off, and ripping seams. From that we moved up to bloody each other's noses.

Tears rolled down our dusty cheeks while each of us was helped "out of the ring" by our respective fans. Off we went in opposite directions.

Later that day we came to our senses and made up, vowing never to fight over a girl again. And we didn't.

XXII

...... DONKEY

(Sostenes Rocha's story as told by Virginia Cordts)

I called my first donkey "El burro Holino" because he had a little "stump" of a tail. I would grab hold of the stumpy tail, step on the bend of his hind leg and jump up on him.

El burro Holino was a good donkey. I just tightened my heels on his sides and he'd start trotting. He needed no reins; I simply touched him on the side and he'd turn.

It was a tiny little donkey, and my uncle gave him to me when I was eight so that I could go to visit his three hacieudas; La Guadalupe, La San Gabriel, and La Poruenier. I was too little to work, so I just went around to watch the candle making, rope making, and the planting on the ranches.

As we rode along, I patted the soft neck of my burro, and talked to him about where we had been, and what we had seen.

I wonder, now, what people thought when they saw me, sitting on that little donkey talking so earnestly to him.

XXIII

. . . . . . DOG

(Robert Wilson's story as told by Holly Wilson)

 was ten years old and my life was complete because I had Prince. He was a mutt of a dog, just a hank of black, brown, and white hair.

Prince and I hunted frogs and he roamed around while I climbed trees. Our specialty was rounding up cows and pigs. My job was to run and yell at the animals while Prince's job was to bark and bite the heels of those critters.

Together we made the best team around.

We were really poor, and the terrible day came when we couldn't afford to feed Prince, even if all he ate were table scraps and milk. A farmer down the road said he'd give Prince a new home.

I had a big lump in my throat as I put my arms around Prince's neck and told him I'd always love him. He jumped in the back of an old pickup truck and I watched them drive down the dusty road.

Prince watched me until they got out of sight, and I am sure that he said he would always love me, too.

XXIV

. . . . . . PET CHICKEN

(Mallie Parks's story as told by Beverly Parks Faaborg)

he air was still, and it was a typical quiet summer day on the farm when I was four years old. Uncle Bill was behind the horse drawn mower cutting hay while I watched from the yard. I certainly wasn't ready for what happened next.

Suddenly the air exploded with squawking and harsh

crying from a leghorn chicken that had been hiding in the path of the mower. She flopped around sending blood onto the grass as Uncle Bill stopped the horses to investigate.

The poor chicken had been hit by the mower and had lost a leg to that sharp sickle blade. I ran and got rags to wrap around her and picked her up, comforting and talking to her.

"It's okay, Don't be scared. I'll take good care of you."

And, take care, I did. Old "Crip" was my best friend. The country farm had been lonely for me. I had few playthings, and no playmates.

Old Crip got better every day and soon we were playing. Now I REALLY had something to do.

When I called from the doorway, Crip would come running, and we'd chase each other.

Other times I cradled Crip in my arms and pretended she was a doll as I'd talk baby talk to her.

Crip turned out to be one farm chicken that never became a Sunday dinner.

XXV

...... COW CHASE

(Lydia Thomes's story as told by Jamie Belcher)

 here is nothing cuter than baby calves. They just sort of look at you with those unbelievabley long eyelashes, and your heart just turns to mush.

One day when I was living on the farm as a child, we had three baby calves at one time. Those cute little things were out in the pasture with their mamas.

I just couldn't stand the thought of them being out there going unpetted, and uncuddled. So, my sisters and I set out across the timber one afternoon to hunt down those cows and their calves.

There were several fences but we were used to climbing over, under, and through them. We knew, of course, that we'd have to be awfully careful of our cotton summer dresses in those snaggy old barb wire fences.

As we crossed the last fence into the pasture we had kind of forgotten how mama cows can be real fiesty about their babies.

The cows found us about the same time we found them.

They looked up in surprise when they saw us moving toward their precious babies, bellowed loudly, and started toward us.

Now, skinny little farm girl legs can just move out awfully fast if their owner is being chased by three one thousand pound cows, so I made it to the protection of the fence alright. But, I got my dress caught on the wire and was screaming as if those cows already had me. The cows were thundering closer, and I couldn't get through the fence. I could just imagine what those horns would do to me if I gave them a chance.

Fortunately, my sisters grabbed me and pulled me on through to safety.

That day those calves went unpetted and uncuddled.

XXVI

...... DAY OF KINDERGARTEN

(George Andre's story as told by Reagan King)

I wanted to be a kindergarten drop out!

One of the reasons I didn't want to go to school was that I thought I was already smart enough, so school was unnecessary for a kid like me.

There sat the little brick school. I didn't want to go. I especially didn't want to walk to school. What if I got lost? What if someone chased me? What if I got hurt?

I had heard stories about the big paddle with holes in it, the dunce hat, and rulers to whack knuckles. I could imagine what would happen to me if I sat in the wrong seat or talked out of turn.

The first day, as my mother got me ready for school, I had a pouty face with big tears hanging on my eye lashes. But, away I went with her to my first day of unnecessary school. People said I needed to go to school to get a job. I figured that was an odd reason since I didn't want a job either.

None of the bad things I worried about happened, and I even discovered that there were some good parts of school. I loved the thing called recess. And I loved music time and gym time. In fact, I even started liking school!

Fortunately, I didn't drop out of school that day, nor all the ones that followed.

XXVII

...... SANDBOX

(Richard Meyer's story as told by Kimberly Meyer)

ixty years ago my mother walked me to kindergarten for my first day of school.

She introduced me to Miss Shack and left to go to visit my aunt who didn't live too far away.

Perhaps I was a little apprehensive about the whole thing anyway. Maybe the bigger kids had convinced me I was going to get in all kinds of trouble, so I was half way expecting it.

But, anyway, when Miss Shack divided the kids up to play and stuck me in a sandbox, I figured I was being punished for something. There, I hadn't been in school long enough to meet all the other kids, much less long enough to learn to read, and I had already blown it somehow, and was being punished.

So, I sat in a pile of sand, banished from all the good kids, separated out because I was already a bad kid.

My solution to the whole mess was to chuck the idea, and to go home.

I figured there was just no hope for a hardened kindergartener like myself.

My mother found me later on our front porch with my head dejectedly cradled in my hands, resolved to grow up without benefit of school.

Of course, I got escorted back to the site of my crime, whatever that had been, and given back to Miss Shack.

It took awhile for me to forgive all the big folks for all that, but I eventually did, and learned to like school.

XXVIII

...... THANKSGIVING AT GRANDMA'S

(Phyllis Dunshee's story as told by Katie Wallace)

 hen I walked into Grandma's house, I could smell Thanksgiving! A whole mixture of wonderful things cooking gave the entire house a holiday scent that I loved.

The large table was set up between the dining and living rooms. It looked lovely in the white linens which were brought out for only special occasions. One reason that we seldom used these tableclothes and napkins was that it took forever to iron them. My mother said it took ten hours. The napkins were very large, and we unfolded them only halfway to use them on our laps. The "good" dishes were brought out only for special occasions, and holiday dinners were special.

My cousins and I went around checking to see what we would have for dinner, although at later Thanksgivings we would know because it was always the same. There was always the big brown jar of pickled herring in onions and vinegar. The baked chicken and sage dressing were in the huge roaster pan. There were blue and white granite pans all over the kitchen filled with food.

Just in case we didn't get full at dinner, Grandma had tons of pies for dessert. We could count on having a choice of gooseberry, cherry, blueberry, and chocolate or lemon cream. And in case the pies were not enough, we had other sweets. She brought out fudge, divinity, and peanut brittle as well as nutbreads.

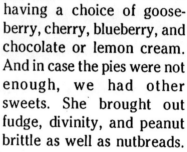

After the feast, we didn't do much running around. We usually visited with relatives and played board games.

Grandma must have thought we still might have an empty corner tucked away somewhere in us, so she topped off Thanksgiving afternoon with a big pan of popcorn.

XXIX

...... CHRISTMAS TREE

(Helen Roth's story as told by Jennifer Chubb)

here was never a Christmas tree more beautiful than the first one I remember we had when I was a tiny little girl.

For months in advance, my papa was on the look-out for a nice evergreen growing in a pasture, in a fence row, or along the road. He told us that, for that year, it had to be absolutely perfect and he wasn't going to give up until he found just the right tree.

Then, one day he announced at the supper table that he had spotted the right tree and that he hoped no one else would cut it down before he did.

Finally, a few days before Christmas, Papa, axe in hand, went to get the tree. Mama and Aunt Rose started moving the furniture around to make room for it in our living room.

Papa brought it up to the house and stood it up for us to see outside the back door. He gave the trunk a shake or two to get the snow off of it and brought it into the back porch.

The tree smelled like a mixture of our cedar chest and a walk in the woods. It was a wonderful wonderful smell!!

When all the snow had melted off and the tree was dry, Papa brought it into the living room in a stand he had made. Mama brought out a box of decorations that looked like magic to me . . . . sparkling, glittering, and shiny.

The very best thing was the lights that we put on, fastening each one to a branch with a little clip. When they were lit, the light danced and mingled with the evergreen smell.

XXX

...... CHRISTMAS PLAY

(Dick Lewis's story as told by Rebecca Faust)

rs. O'Ferrill (our teacher) always wrote, directed, and produced the grade school Christmas programs. Broadway productions had nothing on us!

Weeks before the big day, we'd be copying our parts, using pencil and notebook paper. We practiced saying the awkward sentences, which never sound like natural conversation.

Our one room school house lacked the necessary stage, dressing rooms and audience seating, but we improvised. A few days before the program someone strung heavy wire across the front of the room and some white sheets got put up to be drawn for stage curtains. Since the sheets were above floor level, you could see little feet racing around backstage behind the sheets. Doing the program on a "real stage" added an element of importance to it, of course.

Everyone had a part. Some little kid would do a welcome . . . a four line poem or something. Older kids who weren't able to memorize either had small parts or else pulled the curtains between scenes.

Mrs. O'Ferrill was appalled if we made a mistake, sort of as if her job depended on the program. She was really happy when we did well.

Everyone looked different the night of the program. Girls wore their best skirts, with lots of red and green. Boys had on knickerbockers and suspenders, high shoes, and long socks. The big change, though, was in the boys' hair. It was all greased down, and slicked back.

The blackboard at the back of our "stage" would be covered with handwritten messages to our parents.... "Merry Christmas to Mama and Papa, from Richard," or something like that.

All of the programs followed the same pattern year after year. At the end, we giggled as we slipped around getting the present that we had collected money for, and presented the teacher with a gift which, year after year, SURPRISED her!

The evening ended with donuts and hot cider so we could visit and our parents could congratulate us on what a good program we had.

XXXI

...... BOX OF STUFF

(Helen Herman's story as told by Jennifer Russell)

hen I was little my family was very poor. I had a lot of friends, but not many of this world's things.

But what I did have, I treasured.

I had a box which was my own private treasure box, and I kept it under my bed. No one was allowed to touch it. It was a secret, special box.

Sometimes when I wanted to play, I went to my bedroom and pulled out my cardboard box. Carefully, I would lift the lid and take out my stuff.

First I pulled out the rag doll I had gotten for Christmas. She was my precious doll. Next, came the jacks and ball. I loved to play jacks! And in the bottom were treasures: dried flowers I had gathered in the woods, pretty rocks I had picked up, and some leaves.

My family was very poor, but I was very rich.

XXXII

...... SLIPPERY SLIDE

(Marjorie Roller's story as told by Jason Tutt)

I was so excited that at last I could go down the big "slippery slide" since I was five years old and was in school.

When we went outside for the very first recess of my life, I quickly headed for the big slide.

I knew the rules:

> YOU HAVE TO TAKE TURNS
> YOU HAVE TO LINE UP
> YOU HAVE TO GO ONE AT A TIME

Armed with all that information, I felt pretty confident as I waited for my turn.

When I got to the slide and was reaching for the hand rails to go up the ladder, a pretty tough looking kid put out his hand and said, "you have to pay."

Well, I hadn't planned on that. I had no money with me nor anywhere else for that matter. So, I got out of line and went over to the sidelines to watch for the rest of the recess. I was one sad looking little girl.

That evening I told my mother that I needed money to play on the slippery slide the next day. She asked me a few questions and then said, "they don't want real money; they only want rocks."

The next day I picked up some little rocks and put them in my pocket. I "paid" over and over again as I went down the slippery slide. Now I knew the other rule about playing on slides.

XXXIII

. . . . . . STUFFED CLOWN

(Delores Collins's story as told by Sara Sudbeck)

I didn't get to see my grandpa very much since he lived in New Mexico where he was the postmaster. But, when I turned five years old he gave me a stuffed clown that had a long nose and was wearing a yellow suit with little kittens printed on it.

How I loved my clown! It was my constant companion and I carried it with me to play, eat, sleep, shop, or wherever I went.

As I got older the clown became grubby and grimey. Mother decided that it needed cleaning up, so she washed it and hung it out to dry.

I actually didn't think a whole lot about my clown all day, but come night time it was totally something else.

Mother finally relented and brought a slightly washwater dampened clown to sleep with a slightly tear dampened little girl, and I went to sleep.

XXXIV

...... DOLL AND BUGGY

(Edith Watson's story as told by Matthew Patrick)

hen I was five years old I was so excited as I waited for Christmas. Would it ever come? I was so anxious to see what was in those red and green packages under the tree that I could hardly keep my hands off of them.

Finally the big day came and I was able to open those boxes all tied up with pretty ribbons.

My eagerness to get those presents didn't really do anything to reduce my expectation of receiving more socks and stuff that I'd need anyway. Christmas was often a time to buy that sort of thing for children, you know.

Of course, there was always the possibility of just fun things in those presents, so I always kind of had that hope.

It was that present from Santa that I couldn't figure out. It was too big and too heavy for socks or something like that, so I was stumped.

And when I tore it open, it sure wasn't socks. It was the most beautiful doll and buggy that I could ever have imagined. That china doll had a little lace dress and shiney black shoes. The gray buggy was just a perfect size for her to lay in.

Betty! That's it, that's what to call my beautiful new baby, and that was the beginning of many, many happy hours together.

XXXV

...... SCHOOL LUNCH

(Marge Van Hemert's story as told by Brandon Dietsch)

hat do you have in your lunch today?" my friends and I asked each other. We spent a lot of time checking to see what each other had, and negotiating trades.

Actually, we spent more time deciding where to eat and with whom to eat than we did the actual eating.

"Pssst, Marge. Will you eat with me today? my friend whispered across the aisle.

So, off we went to find a private spot. We had big secrets to tell, and we couldn't do that on the front steps with everyone else.

One of the very best places was up in the trees, but the boys had those places already.

We took off running, swinging our lunch buckets . . . a syrup can, Grandpa's Prince Albert or his Velvet tobacco can. We had to be careful that we didn't break the glass canning jars that held our messy stuff.

We checked out the other good lunch spots. Some kids already had settled on the side of the ditch under the trees where the big roots were perfect for sitting on. We'd have to look somewhere else.

With eager eyes and chubby little hands we checked to see what each other had: I often brought some canned beef, or peanut butter and jelly sandwiches. Sometimes we had fried chicken or dried beef. The really special treat was discovering cake in my bucket. The worst thing was to find a fried egg sandwich in my lunch... I made every effort to trade those sandwiches away, almost at any cost.

On we went, hunting for a good spot to eat. Other kids had the teeter-totter and the swings. Someone was on the end of the slide. Even the concrete slab by the pump was taken.

We heard one of the boys hollering to the others to be sure to save the waxed paper for the slide. Using a little of that waxy paper would make that slide go a lot faster.

At last we came to just the right spot. No one had decided to eat there this day, and it was ours alone. The coal house was all ours!

XXXVI

. . . . SCHOOL BOX SOCIAL

(Ruth Kempf's story as told by Eric Ryner)

xcitment was running high at the school. The teacher had gotten there early in her buggy and two dozen of us students came bursting in soon after.

The girls whispered and giggled a lot. The boys alternated between worried looks and knowing whispers.

The teacher called, "third grade arithmetic come forward." The two or three third graders went to the front of the room and sat by the teacher's desk on a "recitation bench." They had arithmetic and then returned to their desks. So, it went all morning.

Recess at last!! I wanted to see how the other girls were decorating their boxes for the social. Off to the girls' cloak room to exchange secret information!

We bigger girls enlightened the younger ones. Rule #1: decorate your box with crepe paper and ribbons. Rule #2: don't tell anyone which box is yours. Rule #3: have good sandwiches, cake, cookies, and maybe some fried chicken in your box.

The bell rang for "books" so back to the desks we went. Sometimes we were able to get the teacher off onto a discussion that got us around our studies.

All the classes had music at the same time. Music was simply a time when the teacher played the piano and everyone sang. That was our music class.

By afternoon recess we began to worry . . . . . . what if some great big person bought my box and had to sit right with me at my little desk bench? What if no one bids on my box?? What if . . . . .

The whole community turned out that night. The girls and the women brought beautiful boxes, all containing endless goodies. The boys and the men all brought pockets full of change they hoped to turn into the opportunity to eat with whoever prepared the box they would purchase.

The bidding started and one by one the boxes were sold to the highest bidder.

Mine was held up and folks started the bidding. A quarter, fifty cents, a dollar. Two whole dollars!

I remember that there was something else the little girls needed to know: It was okay to nudge someone when your box is up for bids and it's okay to tell someone special what your box looks like.

XXXVII

...... CHINA DOLL

(Halcyon Gawthorp's story as told by Michelle Phillips)

April 9, 1926 was a bright and sunny day. And, it was a real special one too, for it was my ninth birthday. Sometime really really exciting was about to happen to me this day.

This was the day that my mother was going to take me on an adventure.

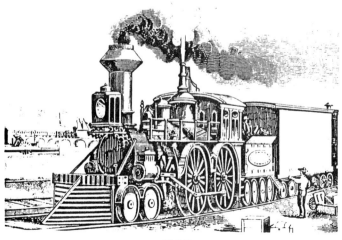

We boarded a train for Omaha which was a long long way from our hometown of Creston, Iowa. It was even in a different state!

My lunch in Omaha just about went to waste, my being so excited about what I was going to get that day. It was going to be a brand new china doll.

My little heart was just more than pounding when we went through those doors into the toy department. There were so many things to see and to explore!

Then it happened! I saw her! I saw the most beautiful china doll in the whole world. She had sparkling blue eyes and light brownish painted hair. She wore a white gown with lace all over it. My mother bought her and we headed home.

But what makes this china doll so very special is that I gave it to my daughter who has given it to her daughter, Michelle. So now, my first china doll is sixty five years old, and my granddaughter is nine years old, just like I was the day I got on that train for Omaha.

XXXVIII

. . . . . . STILTS

(Ethel Gieselman's story as told by Amanda Donlan)

ow high on that board did we dare nail the foot rest? If it was too high and I fell, it would be that much father to fall than if we nailed it low down.

But courage overcame good sense and we nailed the little foot rests on those homemade stilts pretty high, about two feet from the bottom of the stilt.

And, as did thousands of porches across America, ours served as a launching place for me and my pair of new stilts. Learning how to walk on them was really just a matter of falling off and falling off until I finally got the hang of it.

It was nice when I had the luxury of someone holding onto me so I could get started, and then catching me when I started to fall. It was nice, but I usually had to start off from my perch on the porch.

After lots of skinned knees and bumped elbows I did learn to walk on those things pretty well. We got so we didn't fall off every few steps like we did at first. We even got so we could race and play tag on them.

Of course, we couldn't let things go when they were going so good, so we had to make new stilts

that would put us higher in the air and dropped us farther when we fell, but it was worth it. It made us feel that much more grown up.

XXXIX

...... PICNICS

(Dora Ross's story as told by Daniel Wisner)

I loved picnics, and my fondest memories are of our family going out for those special treats. I guess I wasn't just but knee high to an ant when I first went on one of those.

Our family found lots of places to picnic, but the ones we had in the woods were kind of extra special.

Mother would spread the quilt on the ground, and we kids would take off to explore. We mostly just ran around, playing tag and hiding from each other.

When the flowers were in bloom, I collected a handful for Mother. They were usually just common daisies or bluebells or something like dandelions. She acted like they were the most special flowers in the world. As I look back now, they probably were.

After playing for awhile of playing we would, all red-faced and out of breath, head on back to the quilt to see what Mother had for dinner.

There would be yummy fried chicken, and apples, and lemonade from a big glass jar. What a feast! And after we ate enough of all that stuff we could hardly wiggle, there would be a pan of homemade cake for dessert.

After eating, we'd lay around on the blankets and watch the clouds for a while. Mother and Pa took little cat-naps. Those were lazy afternoons.

Getting caught in the summer rain was even fun. We huddled under trees or our blankets to wait for it to stop . . . . then back to our playing.

It would be one bunch of tired kids that would crawl into their beds that night.

XL

...... WOODPECKER CHURCH

(Edna Moss's story as told by Haddi Bergstrom)

he most faithful of our regulars were in attendance as usual. And, as usual, they were pecking . . . pecking . . . pecking.

I wondered if those woodpeckers were sent by the Lord. They seemed to have such a sense of mission about them. They would nest in the cupola of the church and peck away so diligently during the services. Folks called our little country church "The Woodpecker Church."

In the winter we bundled up to ride to "The Woodpecker Church" in a bobsled. The two horses pranced over the snow-covered roads with as many as fifteen people, cozy as we sat on robes spread out on new hay.

And, we could almost feel our tummies getting warm already from the oyster stew supper we'd have at the church.

Since the church had only one room, the pews were pushed aside and the tables set up around the big wood heating stove.

We had those socials every month so the farm families could get together. When it was cold we had suppers or ice cream socials. I liked it when the men chopped ice from the creek and hand cranked the ice cream freezers. It was fun to watch as one of the men would lick down the dasher when it was pulled from the freezer . . . . it was sort of a ceremony.

During the summer we had picnics in the church yard . . . anything to get out of the hot building. We ran around under the grove of trees while the mothers set out food on long tables. That was really a treat after sitting through the long service fanning with cardboard fans. The fans always had religious pictures on one side and an advertisement for a local funeral home on the other. Actually, they were kind of depressing looking.

XLI

······ FUNERAL

(Gertrude Blaufuss's story as told by James Nupp)

y father was a preacher and spent a lot of years preaching in one little country church after another.

Part of his work was to hold funerals for folks, of course. That was simply one of the things that preachers had to do.

Funerals back then were kind of different because the casket would be taken to the home of the family to set in the parlor for a couple of days. There, the folks could come to pay their respects to the departed.

Relatives and friends of the family would bring lots and lots of things to eat for all the company. That way the people in the family didn't have to do any cooking and such.

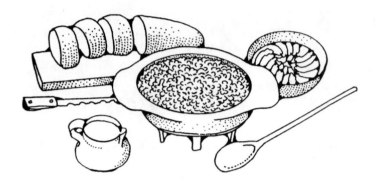

Maybe I was wrong, but it seemed to me that folks that would come to pay their respects always seemed to be awfully hungry. I do know that a lot of food got put away during those "parlor visits."

I would often get in on that part of the funerals, but didn't go to the actual burying. That is, I didn't go to the burying until they had a funeral for a little girl about my age.

My parents decided that it would be a good idea for me to go to the burying for that one.

So, I went, not willingly, but I went.

I stood there on the green grass of the little church cemetery, not really knowing what to expect from this burying part of a funeral.

The grave had been dug by hand by a couple of the men in the church and you could see the gaping hole in the ground and the huge pile of dirt piled up beside it.

The plan was that we could all stand there while some men shoveled the dirt back down into that hole, on top of the casket.

Everything was going pretty well for a burying that I hadn't wanted to go to in the first place.

That is, everything seemed to be going pretty well until the men started to throw that dirt down onto the casket. I stood there in the lawn, biting my lip painfully as I was worried sick that putting all that dirt down onto the casket would smother the poor little girl inside.

XLII

. . . . . . ICE STORM

(Harriet Redwine's story as told by Kim Hood)

y sister, Doris, and I could hear the sleet on the roof as we huddled under the piles and piles of quilts. We tried to sleep as the wind rattled the windows. And, we sure tried to convince ourselves that it wasn't really a day of school, and we wouldn't really have to trudge through the winter day to go to school again, would we??

But we had to. We put on clothes on top of clothes, then finally strapped on some "ice creepers" over our shoes. Our mother told us that the school was there, the school teacher was there, and we were going to be there, too.

Outside, the countryside looked like a day of magic. Everything was changed by the ice storm! The sunshine caused all the ice-coated weeds to glitter like diamonds, and trees were all sparkling. Lots of the heavy limbs and broken off under the weight of the ice and lots of tree trunks were splitting apart from those heavy heavy limbs.

Doris and I started the two mile walk to our country school. It must have been funny to see us, slipping around with arms flying this way and that. Our feet were of a mind of their own, making us do a kind of dance that hadn't been invented yet. We hung onto each other and were up and down .... mostly down ... until we came to the fence.

No matter how we tried, there was simply no crossing that fence, so we danced our way back to the house.

We were a little concerned about what our mother would say when we came back, not having gone to school. That was a pretty serious affair, not going to school that way.

We were pretty glad to find that our mother was relieved that we had turned back rather than gone on to school through all that ice.

XLIII

. . . . . . GLASSES

(Phoebe Hull's story as told by Arthur Carkuff)

lasses!! Glasses!! I couldn't imagine it, but that's what my mother was telling me. I was going to have to wear glasses. I just couldn't imagine what it would be like to wear those funny looking things right there on my face, some funny looking things that weren't even part of me!

"But, little kids don't wear glasses!" I said.

But I was told that I was one little kid that would be doing just that.

I was worried about what people would say when they saw me wearing glasses. Would they tease me and call me names?

The terrible day finally came when I was to get my glasses. They were funny looking things, just like I knew they would be. They had little skinny wire frames that looked way too flimsy to hold together those thick pieces of glass that made things look all funny under them as they lay there on the oil cloth table top.

People, indeed, did comment on my glasses. Everybody, but everybody commented on my

glasses. They would kind of look at them and point at my glasses, as if I didn't know they were there. They mostly told me that I looked "different in glasses".

I wasn't sure if I wanted to "look different" or not, but I found that I didn't really care what folks said about those glasses.

For, I discovered that I could see!! I mean, really see!

It didn't take me long to get used to those glasses, and to learn to like them a lot for what they did for me.

I hadn't realized that the leaves on the trees weren't really a fuzzy mass of green, but were actually all separate and I could tell one from the other.

I discovered that brick walls weren't just a reddish blur, but I could see each and every brick.

XLIV

. . . . . . JOB

(Elsie Zachmeyer's story as told by Lea Sawyer)

ow, Elsie, don't fall asleep on the job." my parents said. I was to watch our cow, and to be sure she didn't get out.

"Well, I figured," it shouldn't be too hard to watch a silly old cow so she wouldn't get out.

But, I did fall asleep, and the cow did get out.

My father spent a lot of effort and a lot of time to get that cow back in the cowlot.

But he was understanding. He knew that I certainly wouldn't let the cow get out again.

But, he was wrong.

Again, I fell asleep, and again, the cow got out.

We all kind of had a discussion about the fine art of watching a cow, and came to the conclusion that I wasn't cut out to watch a cow to be sure she didn't get out.

I was relieved when it was decided that I would be better at doing odd jobs at the general store than at watching the cow.

Same song, second verse. I no sooner got started on that job in the general store but what I broke open a bag of wheat and knocked things off of a shelf.

So, it was back home and ... "Now this time, when you watch the cow, Elsie ...."

XLV

...... STAY IN THE HOSPITAL

(Pat Champagne's story as told by Tim Champagne)

Maybe I should call this story "THE DAY I LEARNED TO LOVE SHIPS."

But, back to the beginning. And, the beginning was back in February of 1930 when I had taken sick with pneumonia.

Talk about a pretty scary thing. I ended up in the hospital.

Hospitals can be pretty scary places when you're sick, not very tall, and around a lot of people you don't know.

Then, if I hadn't had enough problems, I got the measles while I was there, and had to be moved to a room all by myself.

(143)

It was while I was in that big old room all by myself that Valentine's Day came.

Now, of course, Valentines Day isn't just any old holiday to a kid, and I was more concerned about having to be alone on that day than I was about my measles.

But, I found out I wasn't alone at all, I found out I still had lots of friends out there because I got fifty-three valentines.

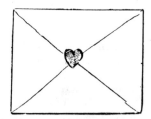

The best valentine of all was from my brother who sent me one showing a ship with some snow-white sails on it, and children climbing up on the rigging. I guess that's why I have always loved ships.

But, I haven't loved cold scarey, basement isolation rooms!

XLVI

. . . . . . TRAIN WRECK

(Frank Kamman's story as told by Robert Sturms)

I was in our backyard during the noon break from school and was just sort of lounging around, watching the men sort out cows from the herd across the street from our place.

I heard the train whistle . . . a long, a short, and another long. Maybe it was that series of sounds that made me think something was wrong, but somehow, I knew something wasn't right. I remember thinking that as I sat there on our porch and just before I heard the loud noise of two railroad engines colliding.

The whistle gradually faded to nothing as the steam ran out. It wasn't long before sirens and bells started going off. People, including me, ran from all directions toward the railroad to see what had happened.

It was really a mess, not the normally neat set of shiny rails with a train parked square on top of them. I had never seen such a pile of twisted up steel, and dust everywhere.

The Burlington train had been switched onto the wrong track as it came in from Washington, Iowa, and had hit the Rock Island train as it was picking up passengers.

The two engines hit head on and both trains had gone right up into the air. When they came down, the bigger Rock Island engine was on top of the smaller Burlington engine. The rails were all twisted around like they were giant pieces of spaghetti.

Police wagons and ambulances charged up the street to the rescue. Miraculously, no one was hurt badly, just bloody noses and frightened people who were bounced around a bit.

Folks just sort of walked around marveling at how no one was killed in all of that mass of twisted metal.

The police kept asking people if they could account for all of their parties, to be sure that no one was missing. They were hunting for bodies, hoping they wouldn't find any.

I was so excited when I went back to school. Since I was the only kid there who had seen the wreck, I was about the most important one in school, not only that day, but for a couple of days afterwards.

XLVII

. . . . . . SNOW SKIS

(Dave Dehner's story as told by Chris Walz)

y friend and I made our very first pair of snow skis when we were twelve years old. We knew that was the only way we could get skis since we couldn't afford to buy ready-made ones.

The first thing we did was to head for the village dump. Someone had told us to use wooden barrel staves, and we knew we could find those there at our very own personal goodies mine.

Since we knew our way around that dump awfully well, it didn't take us long to locate a wooden barrel that we could knock a few stave out of.

Those smoothly curved pices of wood were really strong and just the right shape. All we had to do was to smooth them down a little bit more, and attach some leather straps to keep them on our feet.

After a whole lot of waxing with some stuff that took more elbow grease than it was worth, we were ready to head for the hill.

There we were, all decked out in our ski outfits, endless numbers of shirts, underwear, sweaters, overshoes, knickerbockers, and long wool socks. We had to have lots of underwear on in case our long socks and knickerbockers separated. We walked off toward that hill with so much on that our arms stuck straight out from our sides.

We had so much on that it would probably have been better if we had just stayed home and sent all our clothes out to ski down that hill.

XLVIII

...... HAMMOCK

(Esther Murphy's story as told by Jeff Brockett)

here are you going to put it? Is it for all of us? When can we use it?"

And, those were only a few of the questions we had as my two brothers and I followed our father around as he prepared to hang our new hammock.

The two trees in the side yard looked to be just right. They were, and the trees would give us some shade. Besides that, it was close to the house.

Finally, our new magic thing was ready for us to try out, and each one of us kids had to be first, of course.

After all the negoiating was over with and we had worked out who got to try it I had to patiently wait my turn.

After what seemed like years, it was my time to crawl into that strange looking bed.

I was only five years old and had never been in such a thing before. After watching the others try it, I already knew it wasn't just a simple matter of flopping down in it like you would a bed.

I carefully held onto the sides and crawled in slowly, since it felt like it was getting ready to dump me any time.

What a funny kind of bed to sink into since my feet and head were higher than my middle.

There turned out to be an awfully lot of things we could do with a hammock. We'd push each other in it, or watch the clouds drift by. Other times we looked up into the trees to see what birds we could watch.

Dreams must be made in some part of your body that makes 'em come out when your middle is lower than the rest of you, 'cause hammocks are a great place to dream.

XLIX

..... TIME WALKING THE RAILS

(Robert Orthner's story as told by Leslie Baldwin)

hat if we meet a hobo?" my brother said.

During the mile walk to and from school when I was six, we had time to imagine lots of scary things.

"I'd hide in the weeds!" I said.

"Maybe some bad guy from a far away land will come and steal us and take us away on a big ship." my brother helpfully suggested.

"Yeah, and maybe he'd hurt us or even kill us." I had to add.

Sometimes we'd hear a train in the far distance and would run up the bank 'till it passed, as it puffed black smoke all the way.

We imagined ourselves hopping onto a boxcar and becoming adventures, traveling to far away lands where we wouldn't be obliged to eat right, get enough sleep, or wear the scratchy underwear our mother inflicted upon us.

We adored the men who worked on the train, even if we didn't know them. The engineer aways waved to us, and so did the man in the caboose. We just knew working on a train had to be the most exciting job possible.

The bridge overpass was our favorite because we could drop rocks down plunking into the water below.

Always, while on that overpass, we speculated about how to escape if a train came along.

Would it be better to run ahead, or to turn back?

Someone had told us that if you put your ear to the rail you could hear a train a long way off. So, we'd always put our ear to the track before we'd venture out onto the overpass.

The biggest prize was when someone would find the stub of a flare or a railroad spike along the tracks. One day Bob found a whole flare and was the center of attention at school for a long time because of that.

It's funny how two pieces of steel laid on a bunch of greasy old railroad ties can open up a whole new world for a child.

L

. . . . . . SUBPOENA

(Robert Gerdes's story as told by Jason Belcher)

here I was, sitting in the witness chair in a real live courtroom! My feet dangled in mid-air as I wondered what was going to happen to me.

I was just as scared as "all get out" when I saw the judge looming above me, looking like some kind of giant in his big black robe.

Was I in a whole lot of trouble? Would I have to go to jail?

Only just a few minutes earlier I had been in my third grade classroom when the Sheriff came to the door.

"I've come to get Robert. He is to go with me."

My teacher said, "Get ready, Robert". She didn't know what was going on either. My heart was pounding and my palms were sweating as I went to the Sheriff's car.

It seemed to take forever to get to the court room where people were milling around and saying things I didn't understand.

I was relieved to see my Pa at the courthouse. At least those people couldn't throw me in jail and not have anyone in the family know where I was. I had that small comfort that day.

"Just tell what you saw, Son."

Well, I had seen plenty. My brother and I were going to school after lunch one day and were excited as we watched a truck crash into a car.

We had been plenty scared after seeing that.

People came from everywhere and asked us what had happened.

I thought it was kind of strange when my brother just said "Ask Robert, he saw it." After all, he had seen it too, but he sicced folks on me.

So, thanks to my brother's quick thinking, I became the star witness to the car wreck.

LI

...... TIME I WENT SWIMMING

(Lowell Mott's story as told by Amanda Christofferson)

"ow, Lowell, don't you dare go near the water!" my mother said time after time when I was ten years old.

And, my buddies and I liked nothing more than sneaking away to the swimming hole on a hot summer day. We'd stop anything, even a good baseball game with the bigger boys, in order to get off to that swimming hole.

We were supposed to be fishin' and, in fact, did do a lot of fishin', using an old boat we found there at the swimming hole.

(161)

But, one day the temptation proved to be way too much for a couple of scrawny little boys to resist. All those warnings from my mother sort of evaporated away on that hot day. We pulled that boat up on the bank, took our clothes off and waded in.

It was a delicious feeling, having the warm mud squish up between our toes. We could feel the moss getting caught in our feet before we got out to where the water was too deep to let the green slimy stuff grow.

It wasn't long before we were sputtering and coughing as we dunked each other and splashed around. We spent the entire beautiful, golden afternoon swimming and feeling sorry for those prissy girls at home who couldn't do that.

As the sun started to go down, we dried off and got our clothes down from the tree limbs. We made sure we had no signs of swimming . . . . . . our hair was good and dry before we went home.

I never could figure out how Mother knew I had been swimming, since I knew I looked awfully innocent and talked at great length about how much fun fishing had been. But, I underestimated her.

She told me years later that she found some moss in my socks.

EPILOGUE

That's how mothers are, you know . . . . let a guy innocently try to lie out of goin' swimmin' and she'll go and find some moss in his socks.

But mothers aren't all bad. The day that Harriet and Doris slipped and slid back home 'cause they couldn't crawl over the fence for all the ice turned out to be a pretty good day when Mother understood.

A person can't help but wonder if the woodpeckers are still whanging away there at the WOODPECKER CHURCH or if Marge and her friend got in trouble for eatin' in the coal house at school.

But, I'll bet there's no need to wonder if Lydia Thomes has a healthy respect for mama cows with new calves or if Helen Coen would just as soon not mess with naked chickens. So it went all those years ago before those pesky wrinkles and grey hairs befell the children who recalled, in these pages,

MY VERY FIRST . . . .

Need a Gift?

For

- Shower • Birthday • Mother's Day •
- Anniversary • Christmas •

Turn Page For Order Form
(Order Now While Supply Lasts!)

TO ORDER COPIES OF
My Very First . . . .

Please send me_____copies of **My Very First
. . . . . .** at $9.95 each. (Make checks payable to **QUIXOTE PRESS.**)

Name _____

Street _____

City _____ State _____ Zip Code _____

SEND ORDERS TO:

**QUIXOTE PRESS
R.R. #4, Box 33B
Blvd. Station
Sioux City, Iowa 51109**

TO ORDER COPIES OF
My Very First . . . . . .

Please send me_____copies of **My Very First
. . . . . .** at $9.95 each. (Make checks payable to **QUIXOTE PRESS.**)

Name _____

Street _____

City _____ State _____ Zip Code _____

SEND ORDERS TO:

**QUIXOTE PRESS
R.R. #4, Box 33B
Blvd. Station
Sioux City, Iowa 51109**

INDEX
(Chapter Titles are in Capital Letters)

A

ambulances 146
Andre, George 91
Andy-Over 25
angel 76

B

Baldwin, Leslie i,153
barrel 149
baskets 50
Belcher, Jamie i,89
Belcher, Jason i,157
Belcher, Jonathan i,55
Bergstrom, Haddi i,125
Bernand, Curry i,73
Bernand, Curtis 73
Billerbeck, Alice 74
Blaufuss, Gertrude 129
bluebells 124
bobsled 126
Bohemian 75
Boughton, Ryan i,69
BOX OF STUFF 103
BOY PROBLEMS 79
bread 49
Brockett, Bo i,59
Brockett, Jeff i,151
buggy 49
Burlington Railroad 146
Burrell, Nina i,79
burro 84
buttons 82

C

caboose	154
cake	113,124
calves	89
camera	51
CAR RIDE	67
Carkhuff, Arthur	i,137
casket	78,129,131
cat	20,49,52
CELLAR	35
cellar	35,52
Champagne, Pat	143
Champagne, Tim	i,143
chickens	43,44,45,46,66,87,88
CHICKEN KILLING	43
CHINA DOLL	119
CHRISTMAS PLAY	99
CHRISTMAS TREE	97
Christofferson, Amanda	i,161
Chubb, Jennifer	i,97
church	24
churn	19
circus	78
clouds	124
clown	107,108
coal house	113
Coen, Helen	43
Coen, Laurence	39
Collins, Dolores	107
Conductor	66
cookies	110
Cordts, Virginia	i,83
cornpicker	48
Corwin, Jeff	i,19
COVERED WAGON	59
cow	85,141
cow chips	61
COW CHASE	89
cream	52
creek	13,14,17
Creston, Iowa	120
"Crip"	88
cupola	125

D

daisies	124
dance	135
dandelions	124
DAY OF KINDERGARTEN	91
Dehner, Dave	149
Depression, The	19,20
Derby, Mary	51
dessert	49
diamonds	134
Dietsch, Brandon	i,111
ditch	112
divinity	96
Doc Mott	67
DOG	85
dog	20,32,33,49,66
doll	103,110
DOLL AND BUGGY	109
DONKEY	83,84
Donlan, Amanda	i,121
Douglas, Dustin	i,23
dreams	152
dressing	96
Dunshee, Phyllis	95
Dustman, Melva	13

E

El burro Holino	83,84
Engel, Kellie	i,67
engineer	154
epilouge	165

F

Faaborg, Beverly Parks	i,87
FAMILY MOVE	19
fans	127

farm	13
FAST CAR	73
Faust, Rebecca	i,99
fences	89,90,135
fight	82
FIGHT	81
fire escape	79
flowers	103
fort	24
foreword	9
frog	15,85
fudge	96
funeral	130
FUNERAL	129
funeral home	127

G

games	59
Gawthorp, Halcyon	119
George, LaShawna	i,77
Gerdes, Berniece	31
Gerdes, Robert	157
ghost	23,25,36
giant	78,157
GIANT FRIEND	77
Gieselman, Ethel	121
gift	101
GLASSES	137
goblins	79
Graham, Lyle	81
gravy	49
Green Rock, Il	73
gym	92

H

hacieudas	84
ham	56,58

HAMMOCK...151
Harper, Gladys......................................23
Hartman, Janelle..................................i,65
hayrack...48
Herbst, Catherine 27
Herbst, Stacey....................................i,27
Herman, Helen 103
herring, pickled 96
hide-and-seek......................................24
hobo..153
Hodges, James......................................47
hog...56,57
HOG BUTCHERING...................................55
HOME IN THE COUNTRY 13
Hood, Kim.......................................i,133
horseless carriage 68
horses..64,88
Hoschek, Dorothy...................................35
HOUSE BUILDING...................................27
HOUSE MOVING....................................31
Hull, Phoebe......................................137

I

ice cream 53,127
ice creepers 134
ICE STORM 133
Italians...27,28
Italy...28

J

jacks..103
jail...157
job...92
JOB..141
Jones, Miss..76
Judd, Shawn.....................................i,81
judge...157

(173)

K

Kamman, Frank 145
Kempf, Ruth 115
kettle 56,57
kindergarten 79,91,93
King, Reagan i,91
knickerbockers 150
Kroeger-Manley, Laura 77

L

lace 120
ladder 105
La Guadalupe 84
lamp 36
La Poruenier 84
lard 57,58
La San Gabrial 84
lemonade 124
Lewis, Dick 99
lime 40
Lloyd, Dick 19
lunch 111

M

magic 14,53,134,151
Meyer, Kimberly i,93
Meyer, Richard 93
MILKING 51
Miller, Audra 59
Miss Shack 93,94
Model T 69
money 106
monster 47
Moss, Edna 125
Mott, Lowell 161
mower 87
Murphy, Ester 151
music 116

N

NEIGHBOR 75
Nelson, Sarah i,35
New Mexico 107
noses 82
Nupp, James i,129
nutbread 96

O

Oak Stubblefield 70
O'Ferrill, Mrs 99,100
Omaha, Nebraska 120
Orthner, Robert 153
OUTHOUSE 39
overpass 154
oyster stew 126

P

parade 31
Parks, Mallie 87
parlor 129
party 27
passenger 146
pasture 97
Patrick, Matthew i,109
peanut butter 96
PET CHICKEN 87
Peterson, Zach i,43
Phillips, Michelle 119
PICNICS 123
pie 96
pig 85
Piper, Damion i,39
pneumonia 143
police 146
Polk, President 23
popcorn 96

porch	121,145
postmaster	107
preacher	129
preface	11
Prince	85,86
Prince Albert tobacco can	112
prize	70,81,82
pump	113
pumpkin pie	53
puppies	32

Q

quilt	124,133

R

racetrack	70
racing	70
railroad	60
raining	124
ranch	84
Redwine, Harriet	133
rib	67,68
RICKETY OLD EMPTY HOUSE	23
roast	57
Rocha, Sostenes	83
Rock Island Railroad	146
Roller, Marjorie	105
Ross, Dora	123
Roth, Helen	97
Russell, Jennifer	i,103
Ryner, Eric	i,115

S

Sacora, Bobbie	i,75
Sacora, Gerald	75

SANDBOX 93
Santa 110
sandwiches 113
sausage 57
Sawyer, Lea i,141
Schoelkopf, Dorothy 65
school 20,91,92,94,133
SCHOOL BOX SOCIAL 115
SCHOOL LUNCH 111
separator 19
Sheriff 157
"skipping rocks" 16
SLEIGH RIDE 63
SLIPPERY SLIDE 105
Smith, Sarah i,51
smokehouse 58
SNOW SKIS 149
socks 150
spooks 79
staves 149
STAY-IN-THE-HOSPITAL 143
STILTS 121
STREET CAR RIDE 65
STUFFED CLOWN 107
Sturdevant, Sarah i,13
Sturms, Robert i,145
SUBPOENA 157
Sudbeck, Sara i,107

T

teeter-totter 113
THANKSGIVING AT GRANDMA'S 95
Thomes, Lydia 89
THRESHING 47
TIME I WENT SWIMMING 161
TIME WALKING THE RAILS 153
train 60,61
truck 20,86
Turley, Brandie i,31
Tutt, Jason i,105

U

underwear 150

V

varmint 36
Velvet Tobacco Can 112
Virginia Street 32

W

wagons 32,49
Wallace, Katie i,95
Walz, Chris i,149
Washington, Iowa 146
Wasson, Jason i,47
Watson, Edith 109
wax 150
waxed paper 113
Wetherford, John 69
wheat 142
whipped cream 53
Willard, Deloris 63
Wilson, Holly i,85
Wilson, Robert 85
Wisner, Daniel i,123
Witte, Winifred 67
woodpecker 125
WOODPECKER CHURCH 125
Wordsworth, Stephanie i,63

X

X-Ray 68

Z

Zachmeyer, Elsie 141

If you have enjoyed this book, perhaps you would enjoy others from Quixtoe Press.

GHOSTS OF THE MISSISSIPPI RIVER
Mpls. to Dubuque by Bruce Carlson .... paperback $9.95

GHOSTS OF THE MISSISSIPPI RIVER
Dubuque to Keokuk by Bruce Carlson ..... paperback $9.95

GHOSTS OF THE MISSISSIPPI RIVER
Keokuk to St. Louis by Bruce Carlson ..... paperback $9.95

HOW TO TALK MIDWESTERN
by Robert Thomas .... paperback $7.95

GHOSTS OF DES MOINES COUNTY, IOWA
by Bruce Carlson .... hardback $12.00

GHOSTS OF SCOTT COUNTY, IOWA
by Bruce Carlson .... hardback $12.95

GHOSTS OF ROCK ISLAND COUNTY, ILLINOIS
by Bruce Carlson .... hardback $12.95

GHOSTS OF THE AMANA COLONIES
by Lori Erickson .... paperback $9.95

GHOSTS OF NORTHEAST IOWA
by Ruth Hein and Vicky Hinsenbrock ..... paperback $9.95

GHOSTS OF POLK COUNTY, IOWA
by Tom Welch........................ paperback $9.95

GHOSTS OF THE IOWA GREAT LAKES
by Bruce Carlson .... paperback $9.95

MEMOIRS OF A DAKOTA HUNTER
by Gary Scholl........................ paperback $9.95

LOST AND BURIED TREASURE ALONG THE MISSISSIPPI
by Gary Scholl and Netha Bell .... paperback $9.95

(Continued on Next Page)

MISSISSIPPI RIVER PO' FOLK
  by Pat Wallace ....paperback $9.95

STRANGE FOLKS ALONG THE MISSISSIPPI
  by Pat Wallace ....paperback $9.95

THE VANISHING OUTHOUSE OF IOWA
  by Bruce Carlson ....paperback $9.95

THE VANISHING OUTHOUSE OF ILLINOIS
  by Bruce Carlson ....paperback $9.95

THE VANISHING OUTHOUSE OF MINNESOTA
  by Bruce Carlson ....paperback $9.95

THE VANISHING OUTHOUSE OF WISCONSIN
  by Bruce Carlson ....paperback $9.95

MISSISSIPPI RIVER COOKIN' BOOK
  by Bruce Carlson ....paperback $11.95

IOWA'S ROAD KILL COOKBOOK
  by Bruce Carlson ....paperback $7.95

HITCH HIKING THE UPPER MIDWEST
  by Bruce Carlson ....paperback $7.95

IOWA, THE LAND BETWEEN THE VOWELS
  by Bruce Carlson ....paperback $9.95

GHOSTS OF SOUTHWEST MINNESOTA
  by Ruth Hein..........................paperback $9.95

ME 'N WESLEY
  by Bruce Carlson ....paperback $9.95
  (Stories about the homemade toys that farm children made and played with around the turn of the century.)

SOUTH DAKOTA ROAD KILL COOKBOOK
  by Bruce Carlson ....paperback $7.95

GHOSTS OF THE BLACK HILLS
  by Tom Welch..........................paperback $9.95

Some Pretty Tame, But Kinda Funny Stories About Early DAKOTA LADIES-OF-THE-EVENING
  by Bruce Carlson ....paperback $9.95

Some Pretty Tame, But Kinda Funny Stories About Early IOWA LADIES-OF-THE-EVENING
by Bruce Carlson .... paperback $9.95

Some Pretty Tame, But Kinda Funny Stories About Early ILLINOIS LADIES-OF-THE-EVENING
by Bruce Carlson .... paperback $9.95

Some Pretty Tame, But Kinda Funny Stories About Early MINNESOTA LADIES-OF-THE-EVENING
by Bruce Carlson .... paperback $9.95

Some Pretty Tame, But Kinda Funny Stories About Early WISCONSIN LADIES-OF-THE-EVENING
by Bruce Carlson .... paperback $9.95

Some Pretty Tame, But Kinda Funny Stories About Early MISSOURI LADIES-OF-THE-EVENING
by Bruce Carlson .... paperback $9.95

THE DAKOTA'S VANISHING OUTHOUSE
by Bruce Carlson .... paperback $9.95

ILLINOIS' ROAD KILL COOKBOOK
by Bruce Carlson .... paperback $7.95

OLD IOWA HOUSES, YOUNG LOVES
by Bruce Carlson .... paperback $9.95
(Stories about old houses in Iowa and young loves they have known.)

TERROR IN THE BLACK HILLS
by Dick Kennedy .... paperback $9.95

IOWA'S EARLY HOME REMEDIES
by various .... paperback $9.95

GHOSTS OF DOOR COUNTY, WISCONSIN
by Geri Rider........................ paperback $9.95

THE VANISHING OUTHOUSE OF MISSOURI
by Bruce Carlson ....paperback $9.95

JACK KING vs. DETECTIVE MacKENZIE
by N. Bell............................paperback $9.95

RIVER SHARKS & SHENANIGANS
(tales of riverboat gambling of years ago)
by N. Bell............................paperback $9.95

TALES OF HACKETT'S CREEK
(1940s Mississippi River Kids)
by D. Titus...........................paperback $9.95

LOST & BURIED TREASURE OF THE MISSISSIPPI RIVER
by N. Bell............................paperback $9.95

ROMANCE ON BOARD
by Helen Colby ....paperback $9.95

UNSOLVED MYSTERIES OF THE MISSISSIPPI
by N. Bell............................paperback $9.95

TALL TALES OF THE MISSISSIPPI RIVER
by D. Titus...........................paperback $9.95

TALL TALES OF THE MISSOURI RIVER
by D. Titus...........................paperback $9.95

MAKIN' DO IN SOUTH DAKOTA
by various ....paperback $9.95

TRICKS WE PLAYED IN IOWA
by various ....paperback $9.95

CHILDREN OF THE RIVER
by various ....paperback $9.95

LET'S GO DOWN TO THE RIVER 'AN . . .
by various ....paperback $9.95

EARLY WISCONSIN HOME REMEDIES
by various ....paperback $9.95

EARLY MISSOURI HOME REMEDIES
by various ....paperback $9.95

MY VERY FIRST . . .
by various . . . . paperback $9.95

101 WAYS FOR IOWANS TO DO IN THEIR NEIGHBOR'S PESKY DOG WITHOUT GETTING CAUGHT
by B. Carlson . . . . paperback $7.95

SOUTH DAKOTA ROADKILL COOKBOOK
by B. Carlson . . . . paperback $7.95

A FIELD GUIDE TO IOWA'S CRITTERS
by B. Carlson . . . . paperback $7.95

A FIELD GUIDE TO MISSOURI'S CRITTERS
by B. Carlson . . . . paperback $7.95

MISSOURI'S ROADKILL COOKBOOK
by B. Carlson . . . . paperback $7.95

A FIELD GUIDE TO ILLINOIS' CRITTERS
by B. Carlson . . . . paperback $7.95

MINNESOTA'S ROADKILL COOKBOOK
by B. Carlson . . . . paperback $7.95

REVENGE OF THE ROADKILL
by B. Carlson . . . . paperback $7.95

THE MOTORIST'S FIELD GUIDE TO MIDWEST FARM EQUIPMENT
(misguided information as only a city slicker can get it messed up)
by B. Carlson . . . . paperback $7.95

ILLINOIS EARLY HOME REMEDIES
by various . . . . paperback $9.95

GUNSHOOTIN', WHISKEY DRINKIN', GIRL CHASIN' TALES OUT OF THE OLD DAKOTA TERRITORY
by Netha Bell . . . . paperback $9.95

WYOMING'S ROADKILL COOKBOOK
by B. Carlson . . . . paperback $7.95

MONTANA'S ROADKILL COOKBOOK
by B. Carlson..........................paperback $7.95

SHE CRIED WITH HER BOOTS ON
(tales of an early Nebraska housewife)
by M. Walsh ....paperback $9.95

SKUNK RIVER ANTHOLOGY
by Gene "Will" Olson ....paperback $9.95

101 WAYS TO USE A DEAD RIVER FLY
by B. Carlson..........................paperback $7.95